Books in the Mr. Winston Boo

Mr. Winston Book One
"Mr. Winston, Go To Bed!"©
Copyright 2019

Author: Loleta Rae Ernst
Illustrator: Tommy Sutanto
Editor: Barbara Burke
Contributing Illustrator: Inna Nastenko
(Coloring Book only)
ISBN: Paperback 978-1-7340798-2-1
ISBN: Hardcover 978-1-7340798-3-8
ISBN: Coloring Book 978-1-9529470-2-5

Mr. Winston Book Two
"Mr. Winston Turns One!"©
Copyright 2020

Author: Loleta Rae Ernst
Illustrator: Tommy Sutanto
Editor: Barbara Burke

ISBN: Paperback 978-1-7340798-5-2
ISBN: Hardcover 978-1-7340798-4-5

Contact Information:

Please connect with Mr. Winston and friends on
Facebook.com/MrWinstonBooks or Instagram.com/MrWinstonBooks and
follow Mr. Winston or better yet, leave a picture and comment from your fur baby!
You never know when you might be asked to be featured in the next book!
To keep in touch, visit www.MrWinstonBooks.com
and sign up on the mailing list.

Purchase Author Signed Books,
Find Out Where to Purchase, or Contact for Events:
www.mrwinstonbooks.com
mrwinstonbooks@gmail.com

PREFACE

Wow this was a crazy labor of love.

One day I had what I thought was an AMAZING idea for book two! Mr. Winston already had so many different pet friends on his social media, and since the book was about shyness and inclusion, wouldn't it be great if some of these very real, and very different friends would attend, "Mr. Winston Turns One!"? So Mr. Winston asked his social media if anyone wanted to attend his first birthday party! We ended up with dozens on the party list. Finally twenty dedicated partygoers lovingly submitted their pictures for the book, likely multiple times, so that we could incorporate them into Mr. Winston's first birthday party.

When I say "We", you have to believe that drawing twenty real pets was entirely possible, only because of the ultra talented illustrator, Tommy. In the end, he brilliantly illustrated each and every pet. He took "Mr. Winston, Go To Bed!" times ten! Thank you Tommy, for your dedication, creativity, and definitely, your patience with me. I am super proud of our collaboration on this book.

Mom, Dad, Sharon, Papa, Kenzie, Valerie V., Valerie K., George, Sho, Ashley K., Gladys, and Mateo, (and of course Stormy for book 1!), thank you. And to anyone else I may have dragged to my computer, or the phone, or by email, to beg you to listen to my story and tell me your thoughts, thank you. Special mention to Barbara B., my Editor. Thank you for swooping in at the last minute on book one and cleaning up what I didn't know I didn't know, and thank you for coming in early on this one! I appreciate you! If there are any edits missed in this book, it's only because I've changed something. Your sharp eye wouldn't miss a thing! Thank you as well to my babes who keep me sane and sometimes drive me insane, Baby Nyssa and Mr. Winston.

I had another crazy idea: what if people from around the world read an excerpt from part of the book, and these were strung together into a video montage? People took the time to do it! And on video, so great! So thank you to Irene in Italy, Rebecca in Germany, Mel and Mirabelle for reading in Vietnamese, Mateo for reading in Spanish, Lola the dog (also in Spanish, though I suspect foul play here :)), Shoshanna in Portuguese, Chris and Maria in Bulgarian, Alex in Japanese! The diversity of the cast and participants of this video really exemplifies what the book is trying to demonstrate. "We are different, yet the same" Where we can truly celebrate our differences and come together yet as "One", as "Mr. Winston Turns One!"

I hope you enjoy your Mr. Winston book. I am so lovingly happy that it's ended up with you right now.

Xoxo, Letty

Special Thanks to the Cast:

Mr. Winston: Letty's adoption from the SFSPCA.com, San Francisco, California
Nyssa: Letty's Grey Cat, Adoption, Mr. Winston's Older Sister, California
Mom: Mr. Winston's Fictional Mom! Based on a Real Set of Furry Pet Mom Problems.
Sophia: Lovely Young Fictional Daughter (Reminds me of my niece Ashley when she was little, with the big round eyes :))

Supporting Cast:

Hummingbirds, Hamsters, Butterflies, Birds, Frogs, Fish, Rats, Bees

Special Mention Goes Out to the Friends and Fur Babies in This Book:

Benson, Orange and White Dog, Cavalier King Charles Spaniel, California
Clementine, White and Orange Baby Kitty, Rescue, California
Frankie, Black and Orange Tortoiseshell Calico Cat, Rescue, Washington
Fred, Orange Cat, Adoption, Illinois
Kitty, Orange Cat, Adoption, California
Lily, Black and White Dog, Cavalier King Charles Spaniel, California
Lola, Black and White Dog, Boston Terrier, California
Luna, Grey Fluffy Cat, Rescue, California
May the Grey, Fluffy Furry Grey Cat, Rescue, California
Mikko, Orange Dog, Labrador Retriever, Adoption, California
Mable, Black and White Dog, Chihuahua mix, Adoption, was California, now Oregon!
Mr. B, Fluffy Bunny, California
Mr. Mo and His Backward Leg, All Black Cat, Adoption, California
Mouse, Grey Cat with White Nose and Chest, Rescue, California
Mello, Gorgeous Yellow Shepard Mix Dog, Rescue, Started in California, Then in Utah
Pecan, Brown Pit Bull Dog, Adoption, Haven Humane Redding, California. Now Oregon!
Rascal, Tiger Striped Cat, Adoption, California
T-Bone, Grey Domestic Short Hair Cat, Rescue, Utah
Thunder, Black and White CRAZY Cat, Rescue, California
Winnie, Brown Puppy, Rescue, Tijuana, MX, Now California Puppy!
Weeman, Calico Cat, Adoption, Australia, Now California Kitty!

All of his new friends
were going to visit,
and he was about
to turn ONE!

"What will they think of me?" he wondered,
"With only my plain white fur?"

He wondered if they would play with him, even though he couldn't sing a word.

All of his friends had so many colors, glorious in their beautiful skin, feathers, and fur.

The dogs and cats
and birds and rabbits.
The frogs and butterflies
and hamsters and fish...
All beautiful, like his
rainbow stick!

They were all so different than Mr. Winston,
in their colors and sizes and shapes.

Mr. Winston was really amazed!

Mr. Winston asked his sister kitten Nyssa, "Won't they wonder when we all get together?"

"Why I don't have any color?"

"Don't worry, you will see, you are still so young. Everybody that comes will be their own different one!"

Nyssa went on to explain, "With my thick fur of grey and white, you don't look like me.

And yet
here we are,
a happy Family!"

Mr. Winston felt better.
He was getting ready
for the big day...

When all of his friends
would come together, and
dance and sing and play!

While at home, Sophia and Nyssa were letting in all of their friends. It was going to be an early Birthday surprise!

When Mr. Winston walked in the door,
his friends burst out and yelled, "SURPRISE!!"

Mr. Winston
got big round
happy eyes!

There were little dogs, and big dogs,
baby kittens and fat cats.

There was even a bunny, plus the hummingbirds, frogs, and rats! Butterflies, bees, and a bunch of birthday hats!

Mikko, a big Labrador Retriever,
bounded over. Energy off the charts!
His fur, a gorgeous golden color.
You could see the love in his heart.

He took Mr. Winston
by the chin and said he
looked lovely in white. And
shared that he should always
love and embrace
being bright!

"There is only one Mikko" he said,
"Just like there's only one
Mr. Winston too!
We all love each other's colors,
surely, what else would we do?"

Lily and Benson came to give Mr. Winston a high five! They were both super nice.

And Lily
and Mr. Winston
laughed about both
being black and white!

Rascal, with fur like a tiger on his throat, danced over with the butterflies.

He told Mr. Winston, "I'm not trying to gloat...

Winnie the puppy
came over with
Thunder riding
on his back.

Thunder jumped
off and raced
around the pack.

Winnie said, "Don't worry about Thunder. Everyone knows he's got a lot of energy!" And Mr. Winston thought, "That's funny! That's what mom always says about me!!"

Mr. B joined in with a bunch of frogs and
Weeman showed up with Benson the dog!
Mr. Mo scooted in and said, "Nobody else has a
leg like mine. But I get along on my own just fine!"

The cats all joined, along with the birds!
The party got together and started
singing these words:

Happy Birthday to You!...

Mr. Winston blew out his candle, and started to eat his cake. All of his new friends got some too, made just for their sake.

The guests were getting tired of all the dancing and play. Most of them had to leave to get ready for the next day.

Mr. Winston was still so happy, he was practically in tears. He was different, but also the same, and he no longer had those fears.

His friends were all smart and curious and unique, just like him!

After everyone left, Nyssa came
over to see, did Mr. Winston have fun?
Mr. Winston replied, "Yes, Nyssa, thank you!
I loved every single one!"

Nyssa hugged Mr. Winston,
and they fell fast asleep.
They really did have...

too much fun.

YOU ARE a-MAZE-ing!

Mr. Winston wants to play with his friend the bird!

Can you help him get to her?

About the Author:

Loleta Ernst is a passionate Children's Book writer, living in San Francisco with her city kitties, Baby Nyssa and Mr. Winston. In addition to books, Loleta sells software, cooks up big dinner parties for friends and family, and loves setting up booths on weekends to share Mr. Winston's books. Always an animal lover and activist, she supports her local shelters and hopes that you will too! Through her children's books, she hopes to be able to uncover themes that affect us all at any age, told mostly through the lens of pets, which helps us to read about the moral of the stories in an unbiased pet-centric fashion.

About the Illustrator:

Tommy Sutanto, when first given pencil and paper, has always had a love for the arts and crafts. He started with drawing doodles, then portraits, and pursued a Bachelor's Degree in Media Arts and Animation in Los Angeles, California. He is a self-proclaimed Nerd and proud of it. As an illustrator based in Indonesia, he is discouraged by the fact that the country's literacy rate is at 60th out of 61 countries. Being able to draw for children's books, he dreams of encouraging kids to read more at a younger age. When passion projects like Mr. Winston come along, he finds it's truly a joyful experience to be able to work towards something that may one day impact children's literacy.

Made in United States
Orlando, FL
01 March 2022

15264861R00029